A Day in the Real World

Ten short stories from the edge of society

by Elkie Kammer

First published in 2013 by
For The Right Reasons
(Charity no. SC037781)
Printers & Publishers
60 Grant Street, Inverness

ISBN 978-1-905787- 72-2

Cover photograph by Elkie Kammer.

Content:

A Day in the Real World

(Autism)

The train slowed down until it came to a halt at a narrow platform surrounded by woods. Achnashellach was a request stop and apart from the young woman in hiking boots nobody got off. She stepped down onto the platform, where she was greeted by an icy breeze. The low winter sun did not yet filter through the dense branches of the pines and spruce trees. She hoisted her rucksack and waved to the conductor, as the train moved off again. Then she crossed the line and strode out into the hills.

Freedom – that's what a day out on her own in the wild meant to her. Freedom to let her mind wander and her body act naturally, free from the constraints of trying to fit into a society made up of people who apparently experienced life very differently from herself. Free from the noise of traffic, pedestrian lights, electronic gadgets and a multitude of voices, her ears were able to pick up the harmony of bird song and the wind rustling the branches, the gurgling stream and the crunching of her boots on the snow. Without the onslaught of milling crowds, overflowing shop windows and rushing vehicles, her eyes could open to the sight of natural colours and shapes which slowly glided past. The air smelled fresh, the scent of tree sap mingling with the odour of decaying pine needles and the clear frosty fragrance of the new snow. No exhaust fumes, no smoke or strong perfumes to spoil the experience. She took a deep breath and relaxed. It was the freedom of the hills that enabled her to cope with that other life in the city. Once a week she escaped to the real world, where everything fitted together and life carried on the same as when it was first created.

Soon the trees grew further apart and the panorama of the snow covered mountains appeared in front of her. Everything looked so clean under the white blanket. It reminded her of pictures conjured up by the latest expedition book she had been reading on the train, and a single word rolled over her tongue: "Shackelton." She had to repeat it over and over again, giggling at the sound it made. She could almost taste it on her tongue, a fresh and healthy taste, like carrots or apples; a taste of alertness, of urge and drive – someone who is shaken awake to follow his dreams.

"Shackelton…Shackelton…" It felt good to say it aloud without anyone calling her *mental.* As her legs carried her upwards on the steep narrow path, the word became a story. Shackelton came alive again and his epic journey across the mountains of South Georgia was re-enacted in the wintry hills of the Scottish Highlands. She was no longer the young lassie with the weird look who talked like a textbook, having an answer to everything related to her field of work, yet not an appropriate word when it came to everyday conversation. No, out here amongst the rocks and the snow and a lone raven overhead she was Shackelton, the explorer.

As the day wore on, the adventures on South Georgia unfolded once more. Faced with a steep icy gully, untouched by the rays of the sun, Shackelton put on his crampons and swapped his trekking poles for an ice axe. Before starting to tackle this difficult climb, he took a few sips of tea from his flask and chewed a handful of nuts. Thus fortified, he was ready to pull himself upwards, step by step, until the gully spit him out onto a narrow plateau. Shackelton rested for a moment, his body bent over his ice axe, catching his breath. This wasn't the top, though. Another thousand vertical feet separated him from the summit cairn of Fuar Tholl, doing its Gaelic name proud, since it meant "The Cold Hole".

Shackelton didn't rest for long. Although the rise where he stood was sheltered from the wind, the cold air quickly crept into his bones. Another handful of nuts washed down with some tea saw him ready to face the next leg of his arduous journey. The snow was so deep here that one could never be sure what lay underneath. Shackelton used one of his trekking poles to test the ground in front of him, to make sure he did not plant his foot into a crack between the rocks. This slowed him down to a snail's pace and the boulder field seemed to go on forever.

Then, almost as sudden as the exit of the gully, the boulders gave way to an even snowfield. Shackelton felt his stomach rumble, but this was no place to stop. At least he was warm again, too warm in fact. He could feel his sweat-soaked shirt sticking to his back and chest, a sensation that he hated, yet this was not the time to get changed. With the sun crawling over the ridge, Shackelton groped for his tinted glasses. He knew how easy it was to be caught by snow-blindness, and with the burden of his stranded comrades' fate on his back, he could not risk to fail in his mission. Onwards and upwards he trudged, the snow crunching noisily under his boots, competing with the dull thuds of his heartbeat and the rasping of his breath. His legs were aching with the strain. The rumble of his stomach became angrier, demanding its fuel. The rucksack dragged heavily on his shoulders, though it only contained the essentials for the day. But the urgency of his climb kept him going. "I **have** to reach the summit... I **have** to make it to the settlement beyond this ridge... I **have** to get help for my friends out on the ice..."

The last steps were the hardest. Shackelton pulled himself up with his remaining strength, when suddenly the summit cairn appeared above him. With a new surge of energy, he leaped up to it and collapsed onto the rocks. Immediately, he was hit by a gust of icy wind. Shackelton tightened the string of his hood. The view down the other side was amazing. He couldn't stop his hands from flapping – their natural outlet when he was excited. Deep down lay the frozen waters of Loch Dughaill, framed by the steep cliffs of Creag an Eilein and Carn Mor. Further south stretched a whole sea of mountains, their snow-covered slopes and peaks glistening in the sun. It looked almost unreal, like the painting of a dream.

Another gust of wind reminded Shackelton that this was no resting place, either. He had to move on, carefully balancing across the narrow ridge to a ledge wedged between some boulders. Finally, in the shelter of the rocks, he took his rucksack off and secured it with his ice axe. It wasn't worth risking it tumbling down the slope. Shackelton shed his gloves and mittens, untied his anorak and shook it off, then removed his woollen jumper, shirt and vest. He quickly rubbed himself with a handful of snow, before diving into his jumper and putting his damp underclothes on top. Once he had zipped up his anorak, he felt a glow of warmth return to his body. He sat down in the snow and opened his rucksack. At long last, his aching legs were allowed to rest and his rumbling stomach enjoyed the longed-for lunch.

Shackelton appreciated his food. He always did, and his body started rocking rhythmically, as bite after bite descended through his oesophagus into his stomach. In the canteen at work, he would have had to watch himself, to keep the rocking in check before someone commented on it, but the mountain didn't mind. It had more important issues on its mind, and they were not hidden from Shackelton's experienced eyes.

Dark clouds appeared in the south-west. If the wind was picking up speed, it wouldn't take them long to reach "The Cold Hole". He had an hour, two hours at most, before the blizzard caught up with him.

After draining the last cup from his flask, Shackelton started to pack up again. He had chosen a different route for his descent, avoiding the gully, which in the afternoon sun would be prone to avalanches. Instead, he followed the ridge around to the north, where his only obstacle consisted of a 50-feet cliff. Without rope and pitons, it made a formidable barrier to the safe ground below, but Shackelton knew that the cliff would be covered in a thick layer of ice and with the aid of his crampons and axe he should manage the descent. In fact, he had almost made it, when a sudden slip plunged him the last 15 feet into a snowdrift. A few inches to the left, the sharp edge of a boulder protruded through the white blanket. Shackelton looked briefly up to heaven, his eyes filled with awe. "Thank you, my God, for looking after me," he whispered, before he stood up and brushed the snow off his clothes.

The blizzard hit when Shackelton was safely back at the path that would eventually lead him into the woods and down to the railway line. First, the wind came from behind, lending him additional speed. Later, he had to veer south, with the flakes stinging his right cheek. He tried to turn his head sideways, but it was too risky on the steep uneven path. Twice his feet slid on the icy rocks. The first time, he managed to keep his balance, but the second time he landed painfully on his backside. "A few more bruises won't matter," he told himself. "Think of what you've already come through since the *Endurance* was crushed by the ice. It'll soon be over." And before long he was there, at the narrow platform with the single sign announcing that this was Achnashellach. In fact, the name didn't refer to a town or village, but to the whole area, the woods and the mountains.

The whistle of the train could be heard several minutes before it trundled round the corner and was waved to a halt by the single person on the platform. The conductor smiled. "Had a good day?" The mountaineer nodded, her cold fingers fumbling with the zip of her anorak. She took her rucksack off and put it on the floor next to the seat she had chosen. A finely dressed couple occupied the table at the other side of the narrow corridor. Glancing at her rucksack, she was surprised to see how much snow had accumulated on top of it, but her brain didn't take in its implications. As soon as she slipped out of her anorak, a mini-avalanche showered onto the lady at the other side of the aisle. She jumped and burst out in disgust: "Who do you think you are, shaking all that snow over me!"

The mountaineer slowly turned round and with great dignity stretched out a half-frozen hand. "Shackelton. Ernest Shackelton, Antarctic explorer." The lady looked shocked and so did her husband. They withdrew to the far side of their seats, as if trying to shrink into the upholstery.

"No wonder they react with shock," thought Shackelton. "Most people are convinced that I'm dead by now." But the shock of the fellow-passengers was even greater when they saw the garments this Shackelton was clad in. Who in their right mind put on a vest on top of a shirt with a woollen jumper underneath! And now this strange mountaineer took boots and socks off, followed by the waterproof trousers. The elderly couple had seen enough. They quickly gathered their belongings and moved to the other end of the carriage.

Finally she could stretch out her legs and take it easy. With a deep sigh she closed her eyes. "Ok, I'm no longer Shackelton," she thought. "I've got an hour to adjust to the other world", though she knew she would never fully manage it.

On Leave

(Dealing with Guilt)

He knew that he was going to be sick, as soon as they passed the site of the accident. The flashing lights, the overturned car, the white sheet covering the shape of a body – it all looked too familiar, brought up memories he'd rather have left behind. Yet he couldn't take his eyes off the scene. Even when the bus had passed the accident site and started to accelerate, he felt compelled to turn his head and take one more look. Strangely, it wasn't the dead body that churned his stomach, but the wreck of the car with a light flume of smoke still rising into the air. The wreck. One minute it had been speeding along the dusty road. The next minute it lay on its side with a column of black smoke swirling towards the sky. A car, a jeep – what was the difference? One minute they were alive, travelling towards their destination. The next minute they were… **No!**

He hadn't meant to scream. The sound seemed to have come from somewhere else. Yet the heads of the other passengers turned in his direction and he suddenly found himself staring into their shocked, anxious and curious faces. The next moment he was sick. He didn't even have time to reach for the sick bag in front of him. The vile acid stuff came out with such force that he had no way to stop its flow. It soiled his jacket, his trousers, his boots, before running onto the floor. The stench made him retch again, but this time he was able to catch it in the bag. He leaned back, exhausted. The other people were no longer staring. Instead, he could hear them whispering to each other. While he was searching for a tissue to mop up the mess, an elderly man turned to him from the opposite aisle and offered him a clean, folded handkerchief.

"Take this, lad", he said with a fatherly smile. "Been a Jock myself. Know what it's like. Falkland '87… Kuwait '91…" The young soldier gratefully took the handkerchief and began to dab at his uniform. "Sorry about the stench", he mumbled. "It's the windy road and that…"

"Don't worry, lad", the older man put in. "That was some awful crash we passed there. Gone too fast round the bend, I reckon. Own fault. Not like our boys out there…"

"Ha, our boys!" piped in a high-pitched voice from behind. "I'd rather our boys did something sensible than playing war and destroying other countries!"

He would have replied, would have given her a piece of his mind, had it not been for the acid scratching the back of his throat. Just then, the bus was overtaking a car with a young family, obviously going on holiday by the look of their luggage on the rack. A little girl looked up, and for a split second her eyes met those of the sick man. She smiled and lifted her hand to wave. An innocent child, like the one… No!

This time, the scream was not audible to anyone else. It reverberated in his head, ready to blow it up like a roadside bomb or an exploding mine. The bus turned off into a small town. His journey didn't end here, but the young soldier hastily grabbed his bag and made his way to the door. The hearty discussion of his fellow passengers droned in his ears like a fleet of approaching bomber planes. He had to get out – out of the bus, out of his head, out of this world.

Stranded in a town he had never even heard of, the young soldier took some deep breaths before heading towards what looked like a public garden. He slipped through the rusty gate and made for a wooden bench overlooking a bed of roses. There he sat down with a sigh, putting his bag by his feet. His gaze was directed at the colourful flowers, where bees hummed busily and a butterfly aired its wings. But what he saw was not colourful. It was grey and brown and black… It was a ruin in the middle of the desert. He saw the barrels of their rifles through a gap in the burnt-out vehicle that gave him shelter. The stench of diesel-smoke and urine stung his throat, while the groaning of his injured mate rang like a broken record in his ears. And then another noise. They were coming forward, out of their hiding place and into the open, their weapons raised, ready to shoot. He had no chance, one against four, and who knew how many more were hiding in the building. If only his mates were still at his side. Together they could hatch a plan, use some tactic of distraction, but two were dead and Alan, well, he was as good as dead, judging by the noises coming out of his throat.

A little bird landing on his shoe shook the soldier out of his daydream. He jumped and the sparrow quickly made for the bushes. Since he was up, he might as well take a few steps around the park. He noticed the fragrance of the roses and the beauty of a flowering bush. Then his eyes settled on something else, something every town and village was sprouting. Slowly, his feet took him to the base of the monument. He bent forward to decipher the names carved into the weathered stone. They were the names of soldiers, young men like himself, who had been lured into far-away countries with the promise of adventure and heroism and had never returned. Like Alan. And Rob. And Big Simon. He sighed. They had given their lives for the freedom of their country. Or had they? Had it not been a game? But no, not when their jeep had been blown up. Not when those men with their rifles ready had come charging at them. Not when he crouched deeper into the burnt-out vehicle, his pants soiled and his heart racing a hundred miles per hour. He heard the shot that brought Alan's groaning to an end, heard their voices and their laughter. Only when it had been silent for at least an hour or two did he dare to move. By then the sky was getting dark. He somehow managed to get out, get away, get back to his battalion, but not before he had killed the girl.

He was lying low in a ditch, waiting for his unit to pick
him up. It was still dark, though the first glimmer of
daylight crept over the horizon. She was on her own,
carrying a bucket on her shoulder, probably out to fetch
water or milk some goats. He knew he was fairly safe in
his hide-out, though if she did see him and alerted her
folks, he wouldn't live long. She was coming towards
him, apparently lost in her thoughts. The chances were
that she passed by without noticing his presence. So why
had he shot her? What had she done to deserve to die
young? Was it just because she belonged to the race of
the enemy? Because of her clothes? Her skin? Or her
language?

Yes, if only she hadn't been singing. It sounded just like
the victory song of the men who had killed Alan and the
others. Perhaps one of them was even her father. He
didn't actually remember shooting her, just the sudden
rage that took over his mind and body, and her eyes.
They spoke of surprise, not shock. No, there was no trace

of fear in her face, only that expectant look children display when confronted with a situation that is new to them. She didn't scream. She just fell to the ground, her bucket rolling away, and then a trickle of blood seeping into the sand.

He tried to shake the image off and, instead, to once more scan the war memorial in front of him. First he only saw names and dates, but eventually his head tilted back and he noticed the Celtic cross crowning the stone pillar. The cross. The sign of the innocent dying at the hand of the guilty. Why? Why was the world like that? A wave of despair rolled over him, threatening to sweep him away into the dark ocean. Just when he felt himself drowning, he suddenly noticed the ring. Like a life-belt it seemed to have been thrown over the cross to save him, to pull him up onto firm ground. He remembered what the ring stood for. Someone had once explained to him that it was the Celts way of pointing to eternal life, the ring showing no beginning and no end. The cross didn't have the last word. Life went on beyond death, and unless one could believe this, earthly existence didn't make any sense. It was nothing but futile suffering and some so called fun that left you empty. But if life went on after death, there was hope, hope for the girl he had shot and hope for him, her killer.

He sighed. Somewhere a church clock struck, making him look at his watch. The next bus would be due soon and he'd better hop on and complete his journey. With one last long look at the war memorial he turned, picked up his bag and headed for the gate. He no longer felt sick and he knew he would make it home.

Nocturnal Intruder

(Delusions)

Something had woken me, though I couldn't tell what. The room was dark, but I knew that as soon as I opened my eyes a scream of terror would form in my chest. I waited a moment longer before slowly lifting my eyelids. And there it was, right in front of me, sitting on my duvet and watching me out of menacing black eyes. The scream rose from my chest, but never escaped my throat. It got stuck, ready to strangle me as if that would be a more merciful death than being attacked by that hideous creature.

Where had it come from? How had it managed to enter my bedroom, with the door and window firmly shut? Had someone planted it on me, smuggled it in while I was out? But where in Scotland would you get hold of a tarantula, and such a massive specimen as this?

All these thoughts raced through my mind within seconds, though it felt like hours since I had drawn my last breath. I lay unmoving, unable to decide what to do. Strangely, the creature seemed to have the same problem. It just sat there silently in front of me until at last I lifted my hand. This was a mistake. The movement made the spider jump, as if ready to attack. I quickly withdrew my hand – and the hideous thing was gone. My first thought was that it had scampered under my duvet. Frantically, my hand moved around in search of its hairy body. Nothing. Just me in my cotton pyjamas.

Slowly my hand emerged from the covers, and there it was again, the spidery legs sticking out from its fist-sized body. But wait a minute… Once more I lifted my hand, and slowly it dawned on me that my movement controlled that of the spider. In fact, my hand was the spider, the hideous creature, the fearsome intruder. I wiggled my fingers and suddenly a succession of giggles shook my body. My throat opened and I heard my own laughter vibrate around me. It was my hand, just my hand! How could I have been so scared of it? Well, I excused my panic, in the middle of the night one might be forgiven for such an error. As long as this hideous creature didn't come back during the day.

<u>Trapped</u>

(Addiction)

Tanya squirmed in her seat. It was third period English and as so often, she had only just arrived at school.

And now the old crow wants us to write an essay about an ordinary day in my life. How daft is that! I'm hardly going to let everyone know what our home life is like. No way! It's none of their business that I'm kept awake half of the night by my baby-brother bawling, 'cos Mum couldn't find his medication. Poor thing was already addicted before he was born! Anyway, it's not my fault. Then, crawling out of bed and finding my sweater and skirt still damp on top of the cold radiator and not smelling much better than the night before! Of course, the washing machine has been broken since the Second World War, and washing your clothes in the sink with no proper detergent doesn't get rid of the stink of fags, sweat and baby-puke. I'd iron them dry, only we don't have an iron right now. It's at the police station, 'cos my stepdad used it as a weapon. It's not the iron's fault, so I don't know why they had to arrest it as well.

Anyway, the clothes would eventually dry on my body. I told Stephen the same, as I had washed his uniform, too, but he refused to put it on; said he'd rather go to school in pyjamas, the loony! I couldn't even bribe him with breakfast, as there was nothing edible in the kitchen apart from some broken crackers and a tin of beans. How's that to start your day with? Well, better than nothing, I suppose.

When I finally managed to drag Stephen out of the house in his pyjama top and football shorts (hope his teacher gives him a row!), the blooming baby started crying again. For a moment I couldn't decide who was more important, or let's say who needed me more. You have to understand, Stephen is more like a three-year old than his true age of ten. I suppose he can't help it. Mum was

*going through a drink stage when she was pregnant with
him, which must have damaged his brain. I'm the only
one in my family who can think straight; sometimes at
least. Anyway, to let Stephen walk to school by himself is
a bit of a risk. I mean, he's been knocked over by a car
twice already. I don't know how many times he got lost,
but I'll never forget the day he went with a stranger. He
was only five then, and if that ancient wifie round the
corner hadn't spotted them he might have ended up
raped and cut into pieces.*

*In the end I did let him go this morning, calling to a
couple of girls from his school to take care of him. Then I
ran back in and found Johnny on the old sofa, stinking
and soaked through and probably starving, judging by
his crying. Of course, I couldn't find a nappy. They're an
endangered species in our house. Instead, I got stabbed
by a safety-pin when I was searching through a pile of
kitchen towels to see if one was clean enough for a baby*

*bottom. That pin was really the last straw. I grabbed
Johnny and stomped off to Mum's bedroom.*

*"Mum, get up, Johnny needs you!" I shouted. "Come on,
wake up!" When she didn't stir, I yelled at her the way
my stepdad usually does: "Take the bairn and shut him
up, will you?" But Mum didn't move an eyelid, even
when I started shaking her and bawling more abuse into
her ears. She was totally stoned. In fact, for a moment I
thought she was dead. Overdose. And the funny thing is,
I didn't even feel sad or scared. I've lived for too long
with the possibility of her one day not waking up. I
sometimes almost wish for it, imagining we got taken to a
lovely foster home where the rooms are clean, the
washing machine works, the fridge is stacked with tasty
food and most of all, we'd have parents who actually
look after us. Just imagining such a life takes away the
nagging fear that always tightens my chest but at the
same time it makes me feel guilty, because I do love my
Mum. I just wish she'd stop messing with drugs.*

*Anyway, the bawling baby in my arms brought me
quickly back to reality. Well, in the end I found a pillow
case to use as nappy and simply popped him on Mum's
breast to suck whatever was in there. Having made sure
that Mum was still breathing, I left them there and
hurried off to school.*

*Of course, I was late. I'm always late and always
dishevelled and always hungry and tired, but who cares.
All I ever get is pitiful looks or deep sighs or stupid
advice from the school counsellor who knows very well
that the Social isn't doing anything for us. They sit round
the table, discussing our problems and write 500-pages
reports, but really – they have no interest in getting us
out of this pigsty. One day, soon, I'll be old enough to
have my own place and my own life and there'll be no
drugs and no booze and no fags and dirty suckers in my
home! It'll be all clean and safe and respectable. Trouble
is, unless I'm pregnant, I'll never qualify for a place of*

my own. I'll probably still be in this pigsty in a hundred years' time…

"Well, Tanya, no inspiration, as usual!" The voice made her jump. She hadn't noticed the crow sticking her beak in her jotter. Of course, she hadn't written anything down. Did the teacher expect her to be mad? She swallowed and took a deep breath. "I can't think of anything," she managed to say just to keep those staring faces happy. "My life's kind of – too ordinary…"

At the Bottom of the Pit

(Depression)

Have you ever been at the bottom of a pit so deep no hand can reach and even a rope let down is of no use, because you do not have the strength to take hold of it? Well, this is the story of one who has been there.

I had been walking in the dusk, then darkness for a while. Gradually, the day had given way to night, the light had faded, the temperature had dropped and the sounds of activity had given way to an eerie silence. Yet I was wrapped up so deeply in my own world that I hadn't noticed the change. My legs had been moving without command, step by step carrying me onwards to a place I had not sought. When had I lost control over them? When had I stopped looking for a path, a goal, a direction? When had I slipped into this state where my will no longer existed, where I was carried along by some force outside myself?

At first, I didn't notice the dark, the cold and the silence. I didn't notice anything, because I wasn't really there. Only when I slid over the edge and began to fall, hitting my legs and shoulders on jutting outcrops of rock, did I return into my body. I felt pain, felt fear, felt anger about what was happening to me. Then, suddenly, I hit the bottom. The bottom of the pit. It was hard and cold and pitch-black. Had it not been for the pain and the frantic beating of my heart, I would not have known that I was there. I had arrived in nothingness, a place like a grave, cut off from life. Yet I was there and I could still feel myself. Maybe for the first time in days I could feel myself, feel the pain and the cold and my heart beating in my chest. I was real, not just a shadow driven by forces out-with my control. I almost enjoyed the feeling.

After what seemed a long time of crouching at the bottom of the pit, a new feeling crept up. First, I couldn't put a name to it. Hugging my body for some warmth and comfort, I wished for a thicker jacket... or a blanket... or something woollen or furry to burrow myself in. I was dreaming of a dog with a thick hairy coat. How nice it would be to bury my cold hands in it! And my face... and to feel its breath on my cheeks and to hear its heart beat in rhythm with mine... Suddenly I knew what I felt besides the pain and the cold: I felt lonely. No, not just lonely, but completely and utterly alone, unconnected to any other creature on the planet. Just me, down there in the pit. No one to relate to. No one to live for. No one who cared or even knew that I existed.

This feeling was worse than anything I had experienced so far. The fear of being taken over by forces I couldn't subdue, the pain so searing that it froze the scream in my chest, the cold so icy as to paralyse my limbs – none of it had felt as bad as this utter loneliness. Trapped at the bottom of the pit with only myself, I just longed for the end. I tried to stop breathing, but my lungs wouldn't let me. I wanted to cut my wrists on a sharp rock, but I couldn't reach it. I tried to break my neck, but my hands didn't obey me. How could I get out of this? Why did it take so long to die?

Suddenly I heard a new sound, one not made by my body. I held my breath and listened. Then I felt it, the tickling of tiny feet on the back of my hand. Someone had come to join me. Perhaps this someone had been there all the time. I let it scuttle across my hand and up my arm. I wanted very much to touch it, stroke it to make its presence more real, but at the same time I was afraid to scare it, hurt it or even squash it and throw me back into utter loneliness. So I just kept still, enjoying the sensation of another creature nearby, someone come to share my life. And it was then that my thoughts found a new path: Where there are creatures, there is also a creator. If life can exist at the bottom of a pit, there is no place for death. And if there is no place for death, I have to look for a way to carry on.

The beetle eventually returned to the rock. I lifted my head and noticed that my eyes had adjusted to the darkness and it was no longer pitch-black. I could make out the contours of the pit and a pale light high above. I could see the jutting rocks which had stabbed my legs and shoulders when I fell, and slowly they turned from menacing weapons into supportive aids. Yes, I could make out a route to the top. All I had to do was to get up and begin the arduous climb.

It took me a long time to persuade my sore arms and legs to move into action. Tentatively, my left hand took hold of a tiny outcrop. My right foot found a small ledge and with a deep breath I pulled myself up. There was a sharp rock which I grabbed with my right hand and another undulation in the smooth cliff to support my left foot. "How kind of these outcrops and splinters to come to my aid!" I thought, and the idea of them being put there deliberately to help me climb out of the pit filled me with awe. Someone knew I was here. Someone cared.

Someone provided a way out by turning enemies into friends. I almost cradled the next outcrop in my hand, wanting to show it how grateful I was for its support.

Something changed during my climb. Each step added some distance to the bottom of the pit and to the cold, the darkness and the utter loneliness. Each step made me feel more connected, first to my body, then to the rock and ultimately to the one who had made both. When the moon finally broke through the clouds above me, it was as if God was looking down from heaven, letting me know that I was not alone and never would be.

I almost felt sad when my climb finished at the top. I had begun to enjoy it, the feeling of connection, of finding support in the right places, of getting higher and higher and leaving the darkness and the cold behind. But having reached the top did not put an end to my journey. Looking around, I was wondering what direction to choose next. In the end, I followed the path of the moon.

It led me into the dawn of a new day, into light and warmth and the awakening creation. It led me onwards, and it is still leading me, letting me know that should I ever find myself again at the bottom of a pit, I would still have to bear the cold and the darkness, but never again the utter loneliness, because I am not alone.

That old bike
(A different lifestyle)

"Look at that old bike, Dad!" shouted the boy, as his father stopped the car at the traffic lights. Had they been local to the area, the sight wouldn't have astonished them. Everybody knew Macaulay and his black bicycle. For the past thirty or forty years he had been on the road with it, balancing his gardening tools on a home-made trailer attached to the carrier, with the handles of rakes and spades touching his feet as he pedalled along. Some cursed him when he held up the traffic, while others admired his tenacity and strength to be out there in all weathers.

For some, he had even become an inspiration to leave their car at home and take up cycling instead, realising that they were in fact faster than the cars crawling along in rush-hour traffic.

For Macaulay himself it was simply what he had done all his life. In fact, the black bicycle with the Stormy Archer gears had been the pride of his 16th birthday. He would never forget the day when his parents and sisters led him out into the garden to survey the newly arrived treasure. By then Macaulay had already been working full-time for his dad, keeping up the family tradition of designing and caring for people's gardens. But that bicycle did not only take him and his tools to his customers. It had taken him all over Scotland: from the Caithness coast to the forests of Dumfries and Galloway and from the Western Isles to the Braes of Angus. Without his faithful bike Macaulay would never have had the chance to explore his country, to experience adventures and to make new friends.

Surely, the wheels had gone through many sets of tubes and tyres. The chain and the brake blocks had been changed countless times, and neither the saddle nor the pedals were the original ones. But the sturdy frame had lasted all those decades and would, no doubt, outlive Macaulay himself. When the lads at the bike shop tried to sell him a new model they met with a blank face.

"What for? What's wrong with my old bike that can't be mended?"

The other advantage was, of course, that Macaulay didn't need a padlock. Everybody in town recognised his bicycle and would not have allowed a stranger to wheel it away. Not that the usual bike thieves felt in any way attracted to the old-style, three-gear bone-shaker! They wouldn't want to be seen dead on it! So Macaulay didn't need to worry when he left his bicycle outside a shop or post office, when he exchanged his library books or saw the optician. His faithful *mount* was always waiting for him when he came back out.

That morning Macaulay had been called to fell a sick pear tree in an old lady's garden. The stepladder and his big bow-saw were sticking out of his trailer while he pedalled up the hill towards a roundabout. Luckily there was a gap in the traffic just as he approached it and Macaulay slipped in without delay. Of course, a laden bicycle does not travel as fast as a car, so before long Macaulay had slowed down the whole flow of the roundabout. Some drivers shook their head, while others hissed a swear word, but most of them accepted that there was no alternative. Macaulay stretched out his arm to indicate his intention to exit when all of a sudden an impatient driver cut in front of him. His bicycle scraped along the side of the car and Macaulay was thrown out of the saddle. Brakes were screeching, horns were honking and the sound of metal bashing against metal rang in the air. Then the traffic on the roundabout came to a standstill.

When Macaulay opened his eyes, he found himself surrounded by people who were fussing about him. Someone pressed a handkerchief to the side of his head, while a concerned looking woman asked him personal questions. She wanted to know his date of birth and where he lived. Macaulay wasn't sure if he should give this away to a stranger, so he kept quiet. He tried to move, but the woman stopped him. "The paramedics will be here in a minute," she assured him, though this information only worried Macaulay more. He tried to look around for his bicycle, but again the woman held him back with her hand. Then he heard the sirens. "Oh no!" he thought, when it dawned on him that the ambulance was coming for him. With renewed determination, he pushed himself up from the ground into a sitting position. The crowds started to disperse as the flashing lights drew closer. Macaulay turned his head, making the handkerchief fall off. He spotted his bicycle, lying on its side with the back wheel twisted and the trailer turned upside down. The stepladder had wedged itself between the car's boot and back tyre, while the blue of his bow-saw shone from its roof. Macaulay wanted to shake his head in disbelief, but it made him feel dizzy. What a sight! And to think that a few minutes ago everything had been well...

A man in a green overall bent down to Macaulay, introducing himself as Kenny. "That's better manners," Macaulay thought and gave his name. Kenny looked at the gash on his head and called to his colleague to bring a compress and a bandage. Then he carefully examined Macaulay's arms and legs and his torso, but nothing seemed to be broken. "We'll have to take you to hospital to be checked over by a doctor," Kenny explained, while he tied the bandage round his head.

"But what about my bicycle?" Macaulay asked anxiously.

"Don't worry, the police will look after your belongings," Kenny replied. "They've just arrived at the scene."

Macaulay wasn't sure if he wanted his bicycle to be escorted to the police station. He'd much rather have checked it over himself before taking it home to his cottage but the paramedics were adamant that he needed to see a doctor. They helped him up and led him to the ambulance. Around him, Macaulay could make out angry voices shouting at each other. "That old bike should never be allowed on the road!" someone roared. "And it's completely overloaded!"

"But it was the car's fault!" came the answer, loud and clear. "The driver clearly cut in on him!"

Kenny assisted him up the steps into the back of the ambulance and the other paramedic closed the doors behind them. Macaulay cast one last glance at his bicycle before they sped away to the hospital.

It was almost a week later that the rider and his mount were re-united. Macaulay sat anxiously in the waiting-room at the police station wondering what he would find. Could the twisted back wheel be mended? What about his carefully designed attachment for the trailer? Was the trailer itself still useable? His fingers nervously tapped a rhythm on his thighs until his name was called. A young policeman, towering at least one head above Macaulay, led him through a corridor and out into a back yard. He unlocked the gate of what looked like a giant bike shelter or an overcrowded prison cell for unruly two-wheelers.

Macaulay was astonished to see so many bicycles in one place, but he instantly recognised his own. The policeman wheeled it out for him. At least the wheels would still turn.

"We can dispose it for you," offered the young constable, "The compensation you're due from the car driver will easily buy you a brand new one with twenty gears and internal brake system…"

Macaulay wasn't listening. His fingers stroked the scratched handlebars, went on to cradle the crooked saddle, before examining the twisted back wheel. He slowly nodded his head. "It can be mended," he said with a sigh of relief. The policeman had meanwhile gone back into the storage cage to retrieve the trailer, the ladder and the bow-saw.

"The ladder's definitely had it," he said when he returned with the items. "I'm not sure about the trailer, but the saw seems all right." He handed it to Macaulay who was nodding his head again.

"As I said, you're due enough compensation to kit you out three times. No need to hang on to the old trash..." When he saw the look in Macaulay's eyes, he quickly corrected himself. "I mean, if it has sentimental value, you're perfectly free to keep it and get it mended. I was just thinking..."

"I'll get it mended," Macaulay declared. "That bicycle is built to outlive me. And it'll probably outlive you, too."

Before long Macaulay was back on the road with his tools sticking out of the trailer and his hood drawn against the wind and rain. Some drivers cursed him for holding up the traffic, while others admired his tenacity and strength. To the boy who had come on holiday with his dad, the sight of Macaulay on his old bike was the inspiration from then on to cycle to school instead of asking his parents for a lift. After all, his bike had twenty-eight gears and he had no heavy tools to carry. Who knows, he might still be cycling to work when he is grown up!

The Interview
(OCD)

Kieran looked at his watch. Oh no! Ten past seven already! Why did time always fly in the morning when at other times of the day it seemed to stand still?

He began to button up his shirt, starting at the collar and working his way down. It had to be done this way. Everything had to be done in a particular way. His left leg had to step into his trousers before the right one. His hair had to be combed before he could brush his teeth. The bristles of his toothbrush must face towards the sink when it was put back into its halter. If he turned left towards his towel, he had to turn right again to re-align his body. If his right foot was first over the lintel of the bathroom, he had to enter the kitchen with his left one to ensure equality. All these little rules were deeply embedded in him since his early teens, and the slightest oversight would trigger a bout of guilt and anxiety. How often had he apologised to his toothbrush or tea cup when his carelessness had left them slightly askew or facing the wrong direction! How often did he have to undress and start all over again because of an accidental change in the order! No wonder he dreaded leaving his bed in the morning and having to face all those demands. But getting up he must, especially today with this important meeting looming only one hour and forty eight minutes away.

Kieran briskly walked into the kitchen. He rinsed his tea cup and placed it on the draining board before reaching for his yellow cereal bowl. It had to be the yellow one, since today was Tuesday. He placed it on the counter and opened the cupboard above the sink. After filling the bowl and returning the container of flakes and seeds to its rightful place he bent down and opened the fridge. His hand automatically felt for the milk bottle. At least, living with such a strict routine, Kieran didn't need to think about what to do next. He had his breakfast, then made his lunch – always two sandwiches, one with cheddar and one with brie – put it in his lunch-bag together with an apple, a banana and a chocolate biscuit and he squeezed this into his shoulder bag. Even at the weekend, when he didn't go out to work, he made up his packed lunch in the morning. It was part of the routine and altering it would be too much of a risk. At least at the moment he was coping with life. He was holding down a job and managed to care for himself. He even experienced periods of calm and enjoyment when the nagging guilt and anxiety retreated enough to free his mind and soul for taking in the beauty of nature or the harmonious sounds of music. He was coping, thanks to his medication, though it was like walking along a narrow ridge: one wrong step to the right or left would plunge him down into the abyss.

Kieran checked his watch again. It was coming on quarter to eight, seven minutes before he had to be at the bus stop. He took his jacket off the hook and – right arm first – put it on, before reaching for his shoes. Just when he was ready to leave the house a thought flashed through his mind: "Did I turn my bedside light off?" Deep down he knew that he had pressed the switch before he left the room, but he still had to go back and check on it.

There were barely four minutes left when Kieran locked the front door, but instead of hurrying straight to the bus stop he was forced to circle the little house and make sure all the windows were closed. They were always closed, but the routine had to be adhered to. Finally, Kieran set off at a sprint and reached the crossroads just as the bus appeared. He showed his season ticket to the driver and went to his usual seat. Once an old lady had sat in it and, to Kieran's dismay, he had to choose a different one, leaving him agitated for the whole journey. Today though, everything went well. He counted the shops they were passing – another compulsion repeated every morning – and looked out for familiar figures, people like him, who started work at a certain time and used the same route every day.

Exactly twenty-two minutes later Kieran stepped off the bus in the city centre and walked briskly towards a modern office block. He entered the lobby and inserted his ID card into a slot by the next sets of glass doors. A high-pitched tone told him that the doors were unlocked. Kieran recovered his card and pushed through into the main corridor. The noise of a computer printer told him that he wasn't the first one in, though most of the offices were still swathed in darkness.

"Morning, Sarah!" he called to a woman at the coffee machine.

"Morning, Kieran," she replied. "Ready for your promotion?"

Kieran answered with a snort. "The work would be fine, but getting through the interview is a different matter." If it hadn't been for his tutor at university who personally recommended him to the boss of this accountancy firm,

Kieran would never have got the job. For over two years now he had been everyone's donkey in this department, even though his qualifications were higher than those of many of his colleagues. He was more than ready for promotion, not simply for the pay rise, but for the challenge of putting his skills and knowledge into action. He was good with numbers, always had been. They behaved in a logical manner, unlike people. With a sigh, Kieran put his bag down next to his desk. After hanging his jacket up and reaching for his reading glasses, he sat down in front of his computer.

If Kieran had hoped that the lists of data were able to calm his mind, he was wrong. The numbers blurred in front of his eyes as he was plagued by the image of his laughing colleagues. They were laughing at him, making fun of his compulsive habits, letting him know that he didn't have a chance to get promoted. "You're lucky we keep you here at all," they sneered, "and we only do it for the fun!" Kieran jumped up. He shook his head to rid himself of the humiliating image, but it refused to leave his mind. "I'll show you!" he hissed, his hands turning to fists. "I'll show you what I'm capable of! Then we'll see who has the last laugh!" Striding up and down the confined space of his office Kieran tried to summon strength for his approaching trial. Yes, to him it was a trial, that dreaded interview with the senior management. It couldn't be worse being dragged to court for a crime you didn't commit. Why wouldn't they just let him prove himself? Why not give him some difficult cases to work out and see what he was capable of? Why did they have to grill him with hypothetical questions, which in his state of anxiety he had no chance to answer appropriately?

Soon Kieran was so worked up that his little office could no longer contain him. He took a deep breath and stepped out into the corridor. Two of his colleagues were arriving together noisily engaged in a humorous conversation. The image of being laughed at took over Kieran's mind once more and he quickly steered in the opposite direction. Not knowing where else to flee to, he slipped into the disabled toilet. There he pressed his back against the locked door and took some deep breaths to regain some manner of calm. "I don't have to go to the interview," he told himself after a while. "I could just pretend I'm happy with my current role and carry on as before."

In his anxiety, the thought appealed to him. Why put himself through this torture when at the end he was no better off? In fact, he would be worse off, having to live with the shame of his failure. He suddenly felt the need to relieve himself. "Yes, I'll just call the whole thing off," he decided when he flushed the toilet.

Back in the corridor he bumped into Margaret, one of the longest serving accountants in the firm and just months away from her retirement. She smiled at him reassuringly and patted his arm with her hand. "You'll do fine," she said calmly. "Think of all the talent and skills you can offer the firm. We need people like you in the higher ranks." Kieran stammered a thank you and rushed off to his office before she could see the blood running to his face. Her words embarrassed him, but they also made him think again. "We need people like you in the higher ranks," she had said. "The firm needs your talents and skills…" Was she right? Perhaps he had been too focussed on the problems caused by the obsessions and compulsions controlling his life and had failed to acknowledge that his talents were given him to serve a greater good. Margaret was right. He had the evidence in his university papers. They were proof of his capability to deal with challenging jobs. Didn't he have a duty to himself and others to make use of it?

Before he could dwell any further on these issues he heard a knock on his door. Kieran jumped and quickly turned to open it.

"Mr MacKenzie sent me to take you up to the interview room," said the young secretary and led the way to the staircase.

A different kind of normal
(Developmental Disorders)

The table is laid. The books are counted. The worksheets are named and dated. The word cards and accompanying pictures are sitting in a pile. The chairs are all in place, each the same to ensure equality. The computer at the wall is switched off. The desk at the other end is tidy. The box with games for early finishers has been carefully restocked to match interest and ability. Nothing is left lying around that could be used as a weapon or missile. The teacher nods her head and takes a deep breath. Time to go and get the children.

The room enjoys two more minutes of peace and quiet. The very furniture seems to hold its breath, waiting for the silence to be shattered. Then they come: Harry, Ross and Calvin racing each other; Harry tripping over Ross who falls into Calvin – a perfect introduction to a fight.

The girls come next, briskly walking to their seats, repeating: "I'm good, Miss, eh? I'm good."

At last comes the teacher with Brandon who can't run because his arms and legs don't obey him properly. However, his awkward gait does not prevent him from chatting away happily, telling some muddled story about a knocked-over cat and a drunken neighbour. With another deep breath the teacher approaches the three fighters using promises and warnings until they leave each other alone and slouch into their seats.

Ross doesn't stop talking. He never does, even in his sleep, so he claims. Harry never stops wiggling about. He probably wiggles in his sleep, too. Thea hangs on her chair rather than sitting on it, but at least she is quiet and attentive, ready to learn and to earn a sticker. Zoe looks very tired. The baby must have kept her awake again. Calvin, too, appears to be not quite with them. Perhaps the Melatonin he takes to help him sleep hasn't worn off yet.

When it is finally as quiet as it gets the teacher distributes the picture cards. Brandon grabs for Calvin's card and Harry throws one of his across the table claiming to be allergic to the colour on it. Thea gives him one of hers, which is green for Celtic, and takes the rejected card instead. Now the game can begin. The teacher is holding the first word card up and the children are trying to decode it and to match it to their pictures. Although they are meant to take turns, the noise becomes deafening after a while and Calvin puts his hands over his ears and slips under the table. However, the teacher perseveres until the game is over.

Now that the children are familiar with the new words, they are ready for the book. Harry immediately flicks through his copy to find the funniest picture, his body contorting into the images he sees. Ross, too, cannot wait to see what the book contains and gives a running commentary of what he thinks the story is about, with Brandon chirping in his own version. Thea is frowning, wanting to start properly, while Zoe appears to be asleep. When the teacher gains some control and the general noise level subsides Calvin crawls back onto his chair and Zoe lifts her head. The reading can begin. Harry starts, but when he is stuck on a word, Thea impatiently butts in. Brandon can't wait his turn, and with Ross' never ending chatter in the background, it becomes hard to concentrate. Anyway, they all seem to get the gist of the story and enjoy its content.

Now it is time for the worksheet. The teacher has to repeat each instruction, but Brandon claims that he still doesn't know what to do. Harry grabs the rubbers and throws them across the table, calling "Catch!" Thea measures the pencils to make sure her and Zoe are getting the longest and sharpest. When everybody is equipped with their worksheet, pencil and rubber, some measure of calm is descending on the room, but not for long. Ross is thinking aloud and spelling out his answers for all to hear. Brandon has started to talk about the dead cat again, while Harry complains there isn't enough space on his sheet to write the answers. Thea tells him to make his letters smaller, proudly showing off her own neat work, but Harry is not impressed. "I'm not writing all that again!" he announces, pushing his worksheet into the middle of the table and swinging back on his chair. He narrowly loses his balance. Slightly shaken, he sits up again, drumming with his fingers on the table.

Calvin had enough of all the noise. Since he can't write **and** clasp his hands over his ears he decides to withdraw into the furthest corner where he resumes his work.

Meanwhile, the teacher is walking around to keep everybody on task. Thea has indeed written very neatly. Unfortunately, none of her answers so far are right. Zoe's efforts are restricted to the drawing of swirls along the margin of her sheet. Ross is nearly finished, though he has to read out his answers, as his spelling does not resemble what he is trying to say. Whilst Brandon is whining for help and Calvin is rocking and humming in his corner, Harry finally does fall off his chair, but he gets up again without much fuss. After all, his body is covered in cuts and bruises as he usually acts before thinking and rarely reflects on the outcome of his actions afterwards.

To the dismay of the others Ross is allowed to get up and go into the play corner. Harry is desperate to join him and suddenly gets down to his work in earnest. Calvin is finished next, but instead of going to the play corner he gravitates to the sink where he turns on the tap very slightly to watch droplets of water forming and falling into the basin. If allowed, he would watch them for hours, oblivious of the world around him.

Whilst Ross and Harry are playing war with Lego (in their hands every toy turns into a weapon) and the girls are undressing the two dolls, the teacher sits with Brandon who laboriously scratches the letters onto his worksheet. "Why am I always last?" he wails. "I won't have any time to play!", which of course doesn't make him any faster.

Then the bell rings. The instruments of war are being flung back into the Lego box. The dolls are hastily covered with a piece of cloth. The teacher turns off the tap and leads a protesting Calvin back to the group table, and when something like a semi-silence is achieved, she hands out the stickers before the children are released into the playground.

The room seems to heave a sigh of relief as once more peace and quiet descend on it.

"Not a bad lesson," the teacher contemplates, gathering the books and pencils into the tray. "I hope the next lot are doing just as well." She puts the tray away and sets out little tubs with toy money for her maths group. "Just a normal day with my special kids."

The Letter
(Loneliness)

Seonag pressed her foot against the living-room floor to
keep the old rocking chair at a steady pace while she
gazed out through the window into the hazy day.
Summer was well past. In fact, it wouldn't take long for
the winter gales to arrive. For now, it was calm and wet.
The last holiday makers had left a few weeks ago and the
sandy beach at the end of the road was once more
deserted. Seonag's was the last house along the narrow
road. There had been neighbours less than half a mile
inland, but those houses were eventually turned into
holiday homes. That was when Angus was still about.
Seonag turned her head to the mantelpiece, where a
framed photograph of her late husband rose amongst
small ornaments and pictures of their children and
grandchildren. Yes, Angus had been good company and
sometimes she missed him so much that she even longed
for the fishy smell of his clothes and his deep snoring

which used to keep her awake during the night. When, nearly ten years ago, their youngest son, Callum, had gone to seek work in the oil industry, only the two of them remained. How different life had become!

Seonag was born on the Isle of Lewis and, apart from a short spell as a herring girl on the Aberdeenshire coast, she had never lived on the mainland. In fact, marrying Angus had meant moving even further out into the Atlantic Ocean as he had taken her to his croft on the island of Great Bernera. Well, in those days it had still been a proper island, but even now the bridge across the narrow channel couldn't always be crossed. Sometimes at high tide the wind would fling bucket-loads of water over the rails threatening to blind the drivers and to wash their vehicles away. But not today. Today it was calm and the fine drizzle that had settled over the island wouldn't lift too soon. Today the bridge was clear. Today the postie would come and have a cup of tea with her and accept a home-baked scone, and his presence would drive out the loneliness that enveloped Seonag's life since Angus had moved on to his heavenly home. The visit by the postie was the highlight of her days. He usually had a mission magazine or some catalogue or advertisements for her, but occasionally there was a personal letter from friends or relatives or even from her daughter, if she found time to write in her busy life down in New Zealand. Surely, it must be hard work bringing up four children on a large sheep farm but, whatever the postie had in his bag for her, didn't matter half as much as the fact that he came and entered her house and shared a little chat with her.

These days very few people found their way to her door and Seonag didn't often venture out to the shop in Breascleit. Even her attendance at church had become irregular since her legs didn't carry her so well anymore. Instead, she would listen to a service on the radio, trying to imagine herself in the house of God surrounded by a congregation of worshippers. It wasn't quite the same, though. Deep inside, she felt empty, devoid of human contact, lonely and sad.

A familiar sound woke her from reminiscing. Seonag looked up as the hum of the engine grew louder. A smile flashed across her face, and with renewed strength she pushed herself out of her chair and made her way to the front door. There she stood when the little red van came to a halt and the postie climbed out and strode down to her house.

"Good morning, Neil, what's fresh?" The usual greeting rang out to him, as soon as he was close enough to hear it.

"Oh, it's you who's looking fresh," came the reply, which never lost its charm. Seonag didn't wait for him to reach the door. She walked back into the kitchen where the kettle was on the boil. After pouring the tea, she battered a couple of scones and placed everything on the table. Meanwhile, the postie had followed her, steadily filling her in about the island news which would never make it into the radio or newspaper, but which was of much more interest to the local people than the politics in distant Edinburgh or the crimes in the streets of Glasgow. The letter he had brought for her lay forgotten at the edge of the table while Seonag soaked up his every word. A sheep had fallen over the cliff at Valasay and amazingly survived the fall almost unscathed. A delivery van had come off the road near Tobson and it took two tractors to pull it out of the moor. A woman in Circebost had given birth to twins, while a young boy from Iarshader won a scholarship for the music school in Plockton because of his amazing talent on the accordion.

For Seonag the postie's tea break was far too short, but he insisted he had to go and finish his round. Seonag saw him to the door and watched as the red van turned and made its way back up the road. She sighed. The highlight of the day was over. The long afternoon stretched out in front of her like a desert devoid of life. Her sore legs carried her back into the kitchen where she picked up the letter the postie had left for her. She could tell that it came from one of the missions she supported, probably thanking her for her latest donation and asking for more. She put it down again. The presence of her visitor was still lingering in the air and she wanted to savour it as long as possible, trying to recall the sound of his voice and the movement of his body. She sighed again. Maybe it was time to do the house work. That would give her something to occupy her hands and mind.

The next day the weather hadn't changed. The grey curtain of drizzly rain still restricted her views as Seonag sat in her rocking chair waiting for the highlight of her day. Several times she glanced at the clock above the door wondering what took Neil so long today. Perhaps his van was held up by a flock of sheep blocking the road or he had to deliver a parcel too heavy to carry on his own and was looking around for help. As time wore on without the familiar sound of the engine Seonag grew more and more anxious. What if he had taken ill or worse – if he had had an accident? Then, slowly, as if from far away, another thought crept into her mind. "What if he has no letter for me? Would he still make his way over the hill for our chat?" She knew that posties were very busy these days, having to cover ever larger areas to save personnel costs. She sighed. Part of her felt angry; angry with Neil for not appreciating her company more and angry with herself for being so selfish. The fact remained that there was no highlight for her that day.

During the following weeks, Seonag's life lost its rhythm. Of course, Neill had apologised for not calling, but he also made it clear that without a delivery he could not justify driving the extra two miles to her house, what with fuel prices rising and time being so tight. Seonag bore him no grudge. Instead, she thought long and hard until she came up with an idea that might just be the solution. If other people didn't write to her, she would simply have to write to herself.

Neil didn't expect to find any mail when he unlocked the post-box at the crossroads. During the summer months there would be several postcards waiting for him, written by the tourists who stayed in the area, but this time of year it was unlikely that he drew anything out of the little red box. However, to his surprise, someone had posted a letter. His curiosity aroused, Neil took a quick look at the address. His forehead creased into a frown. Puzzled, he gazed up the road, then shook his head. It didn't make sense. Who would write a letter to Seonag MacDonald and put it in this box, barely two miles from her house? Did the old lady have a secret admirer? No, it didn't make sense, but he'd better do his duty. He locked the post-box and carried the letter to his van.

It was only after Neil had taken the third letter addressed to Seonag out of the post-box at the crossroads that he put two and two together. Of course, why hadn't he thought of that! But no, did his daily visits really mean so much to her that she wrote letters to herself and dragged her aching legs along the road to the nearest post-box? He shook his head, as he knew the answer to his question.

The next day, when the two of them were nursing a cup of tea in Seonag's kitchen, the postie came out with a piece of news that made Seonag blush.

"I just heard from a colleague that he doesn't only deliver letters, but also picks up mail directly from the house where people live more than a mile away from the nearest post-box." He took a sip of tea before continuing: "I think it is a good idea, especially with winter approaching." When he saw the colour rush into Seonag's face, he quickly added: "Of course, letters are private, so I'll not look at the address. The boys at the sorting office can do that once I hand my mail bag over."

And so it happened that Seonag and Neil were back to their daily tea break, the highlight of Seonag's life, and it was the postie who one morning found her peacefully asleep in her rocking chair with her heart no longer beating.

When the shock had worn off and the doctor and the minister were attending to her empty shell, Neil looked at the last letter in Seonag's writing which he had come to deliver today. After a minute or two, he did what he had never done before, breaking the code of practise to which every conscientious postie adhered. He opened the envelope and took out the scrap of paper that had been placed inside. When he read the few words written on it, tears welled up in his eyes, though he wasn't sure if they were tears of grief or of gratefulness or maybe both.

"This letter ensures the highlight of my day. Seonag."

Dog-biscuits

(Homelessness)

It was cold – no, freezing! An icy wind ripped through the park and through my tattered clothes. I had to keep moving or my feet went numb. Burying my hands in the pockets of my threadbare jacket, I bent into the wind. "Just keep moving", I told myself. "Just keep moving…"

I had lived in the park all summer, ever since I had been discharged from hospital with nowhere to return to. My family wouldn't let me back in. My job had been given to someone else. After all, four months in hospital was a long time. And not just any hospital. Well, if it had been a broken leg or cancer or something like that, people might have had sympathy, but mental illness? Wasn't that the same as madness? No, such people one did better not associate with.

Anyway, it had been summer, and a nice summer at that. The park was beautiful with all its flowers and different trees, and for the night I had my den where I felt snug and safe. Washing was no problem, as I loved to swim in the river, and the public toilets were always open and reasonably clean. Even food was plenty, what with all those picnic sites and people leaving half of their feast behind on the grass or in the bins. Yes, it had been all right during the summer.

But not now. The weather had turned cold and wet. The tourists had gone home and the picnickers stayed in their houses. Only the hardy dog walkers still kept coming regularly, but they wouldn't leave any food behind. Yes, I was hungry as well as cold. Freezing and starving. I was getting desperate. Even washing in the river became torture, so I stopped it, and one day they locked the public toilets for good. End of season. The park needed a rest from the hordes of invading humans. Only I was left behind; and the dog walkers.

That's why I found the dog-biscuits. First I tossed the packet away, thinking it was empty. Then I saw them, two bone-shaped biscuits that had been hiding in the corner and were thrown out when I turned the packet upside down. Dog-biscuits. I didn't pay them much attention until I had rummaged to the bottom of the bin without finding a single crumb of food. With a sigh I turned round and fixed my eyes on the two brown shapes at my feet. Dog-biscuits. Could humans eat such things? I had heard of poor people eating tinned dog-food. I assumed what was digestible for dogs must hold some nourishment for humans too. I wasn't so sure about the taste though. Anyway, on the brink of starvation you don't have the luxury to care about taste. Beggars can't be choosers. So I bent down and picked those biscuits up.

The taste wasn't too bad, actually. Something like savoury crackers, and I chewed them well to make the most of my sparse meal. What happened next is a bit of a mystery to me. I remember laughing, then barking like a dog. Yes, I thought I had turned into a dog. I started running and jumping for imaginary sticks. Soon my body felt warmer. I could feel the fur growing all over me and went down on all fours, sniffing the earth. For a while I was happy, almost ecstatic in my new life as a dog but it didn't last long. My stomach was still growling with hunger, and as soon as the rain started, my new-found warmth disappeared. "I might be a dog", I thought, "but I'm still homeless. A stray dog that doesn't belong to anyone." Those must have been my last thoughts before I drifted into a feverish sleep.

At some point, I recognised a man and a lady in uniform bend over me. They were not police, I could tell, but something official. "Ah, finally the SSPCA has come to pick me up", I thought. "They'll take me to one of their Rescue Centres and look after me." My eyes closed and my mind drifted away again. Part of me registered the arms that took hold of my shivering body. My feet touched the ground and I staggered between them out of the park. It seemed a long journey, though time no longer mattered to me. Finally, I was hit by a wave of hot air. We were entering a building, the kennels, I assumed. I listened for the barking of my new companions, and sure enough, they were making such a racket that it hurt my ears. Then I was led to a quieter place. Someone stripped my wet fur off and rubbed me with a towel. New fur was put on me before I was allowed to curl up in a clean smelling doggy-bed.

The following days were the best of my life. The Rescue people came in and out of my kennel to feed me hot drinks and tasty soup. They spoke soothingly to me and patted my shoulder. They even changed my bed when I had messed it up with my sweat and urine. They cared for me. They brought me back to life. I wanted to lick their hands to show my appreciation, but somehow I was too weak for even such a small gesture.

My strength returned with every hour though, and, bit by bit, I was able to sit up, then stand up and walk about again. One day I was stroking my soft grey fur, wondering what type of dog I would be classified as, when one of the Rescue people came in and started to talk to me. First his words didn't make much sense. After all, I was a dog. But something about the man's uniform intrigued me. There was writing on his shirt pocket, like a name. Only, it didn't say "SSPCA". Instead, I read the words "Salvation Army". Confused, I looked the man up and down. It was then that I began to understand what he was saying. He wanted to know my name and where I came from and how long I had lived in the park. In the beginning I struggled for words. I hadn't spoken for so long and the last sounds escaping my throat had been barks but the man was patient and kind. He brought me back into the land of humans, though I wasn't sure if I wanted to return there.

I stayed with the Salvation Army for almost three months. It was a kind of Rescue Centre for strays like me. It was warm and I had enough to eat. But even more importantly, I was amongst people who cared. They found me a place in supported accommodation and voluntary work, which made me feel useful again.

Funny, the voluntary work took me to the SSPCA Rescue Centre where I helped cleaning the kennels and walking and feeding the dogs. One day, an elderly couple came in looking for a West Highland terrier or something similar. I took them to the kennels with the small dogs, and what did the woman draw out of her handbag? A packet of dog-biscuits, small, brown and bone-shaped. I felt my heart miss a beat. The memory of a starved lonely creature crept into my mind. I could almost taste the savoury crumbs on my tongue before I took a deep breath and said: "We all need a home; every single one of us."

If you enjoyed reading these stories, you might be interested in other books from the author.

The Grave in the Mountains (1999) is the gripping story of a teenage boy searching for his missing father in the mountains of Glencoe. It follows the struggle of a young person not only with the elements of nature, but with life and death and with God. Very authentic and fast moving, showing the author's familiarity with every bit of the inner and outer terrain.

Discovering Who I Am – *Growing up in the sensory world of Asperger Syndrome* (2007) gives an insight into the unique experience of life from the perspective of someone with Asperger Syndrome. It recalls the struggles and misunderstandings faced within her family and in education, employment and life in general, the associated mental health problems and how in spite of or because of her experiences she has been able to understand and help others with ASD. Elkie now lives in Inverness and works with children with developmental disorders in mainstream schools. According to Dr. Jackie Ravet (University of Aberdeen), "her story is immensely moving and sometimes almost painful. Yet ultimately, it is a story of triumph and transformation."

Each book can be purchased for a cheque of £10 (incl. p&p.) made payable to the author and sent to Brandon Press, 2 Lodge Road, Inverness, IV2 4NW.